Animals
in the
Rain Forest
by Margie Sigman

★ Strategy Focus

As you read, **predict** the animal you will see on the next page.

HOUGHTON MIFFLIN   BOSTON

Story Vocabulary

boa

caterpillar

eyed

eyes

iguanas

katydid

macaw

moves

poisonous

tongue

toucan

Who has these eyes?

white-eyed katydid

A katydid!

Who has this tongue?

An iguana!

Who has these stripes?

poisonous
caterpillar

A caterpillar!

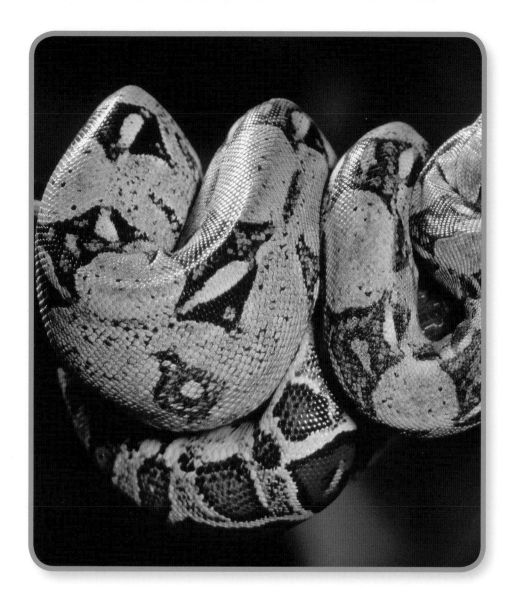

Who moves like this?

A boa!

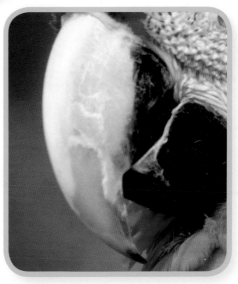

Who has these beaks?

toucan

macaw

A toucan and a macaw!